T0197474

# Petunia's Garden

## Daniel Silverhawk

To order additional copies of this book, contact:
Xlibris
844-714-8691
www.Xlibris.com
Orders@Xlibris.com

ISBN:    Softcover            978-1-6698-2176-2
         EBook                978-1-6698-2177-9

Print information available on the last page

Rev. date:    03/28/2023

## Acknowledgements:

*Special thanks to my all my good friends like my dear friend Olivia Revier, who has masterfully illustrated this book. ovrevier@gmail.com*

*Thank you Sarah W. for your inspiration. Sarah is the adoptive parent of Petunia. Petunia is a miniature potbelly pig, and a rescue pet.*

*Thank you readers!*
*Your support is so encouraging!*

**More books by Daniel Silverhawk:**

The Puppy in Disguise
A Fish Who had a Wish
The Old Pond Slums

Once upon a time in a house not too big,
lived a lovely young lady, and the lady was a pig.

She took pride in herself, and she kept herself clean.
She never wallowed in the mud like other pigs she had seen.

Her name was Petunia, like the flowers she grew
In a beautiful little garden, and in her house too.

When Petunia was a piglet
and growing up fast
Her mother taught
her lessons in hopes
they would last

Like finding beauty
in ashes and joy
through her tears,
And making every effort
to conquer her fears.

She was rewarded for her efforts making her life a fairy tale:
With seedlings to plant a garden, and grow blossoms to avail.

She spent hours in her garden, digging up ugly weeds,
And she carried buckets of water for her new thirsty seeds.

It was a lot of hard work to keep the garden maintained,
But the many colorful flowers brought a joy that remained.

With every flower that she planted, she would
practice what she learned; And she grew a beautiful
garden with the seedlings that she earned.

She sang songs to her flowers and to the blossoms and blooms,
Then brought the flowers inside to add color to her rooms.

She grunted and she snorted and she sang all day long,
And she loved to play the flute to her favorite song.

She learned to play the piano, the clarinet, and the sax.
And she played music for her flowers because it helped her relax.

She played beautiful music for those beautiful plants.
If they could only grow legs, she would ask them to dance.

Her neighbors often told her, she was so precious and smart,
But Petunia only smiled and pondered love in her heart.

Until one summer day when
the farmer stopped by,
And took Petunia from her home,
and put her in a pigsty.

It was a muddy pigpen built
with lumber and straw.
There was no beautiful garden
and no colors she saw.

There was mud in the yard,
and mud on her bed,
There was mud in her ears,
on her snout, and her head.

There was so much gooey mud,
she stayed dirty all day;
And no matter how much she washed;
the mud wouldn't go away.

Petunia missed her little house, and she missed her little garden,
But she kept her hope alive, so her heart wouldn't harden.

When the farmer came to see her, he could tell the move was hard;
So, he bought a bouquet of flowers and put them out in her yard.

She sang a little song, which sounded more like a squeal;
But Petunia wouldn't let that change how she would feel.

She tried to grow a garden planting fresh seeds in a row,
But the mud was too thick for pretty flowers to grow.

So she dug a large hole to save her dreams underground,
But, the deeper that she dug, the more colors she had found!

She found a patch of
green grass under the
bright yellow hay,
And specks of white rock
scattered throughout a red clay

She mixed the yellow
from hay with the red
clay that she found
And made the color
orange and painted
the walls all around.

Petunia began mixing colors, any mixture she could think,
She could add a little white rock, to turn the red into pink!

The mud was so dark she tried to paint it bright red,
And discovered a new color, so she painted her bed.

She painted beautiful flowers on the fences and the gate;
She used the flowers in her memory, to paint and create!

Orange flowers, and red flowers, and bright yellow flowers too;
Purple flowers, pink flowers, white flowers, and blue.

Now she had beautiful flowers of every color, type, and size,
And she began to love her garden, when she saw the sunrise.

Her new garden was perfect, and the new colors didn't fade,
And she didn't have to work hard to maintain
the garden that she made.

So, if you ever have to move to a new house, or new town,
Don't let the lack of pretty flowers, or the thick mud get you down.

Even if you're feeling a little timid or scared,
Keep your dream alive like a treasure to be shared.

Or, if you're in a situation that is dreary and bleak,
Take a look around you, and create the life that you seek!

And if the neighbors that you love, and your friends have to part,
Keep the joy you once pondered, and you will find it in your heart...

...you will discover many colors in the places where you go;
And paint yourself a garden where your dreams are sure to grow.

...the beginning

Printed in the United States
by Baker & Taylor Publisher Services